Gustav Holst (left) and Ralph Vaughan Williams on one of their occasional country walks together, in the Malvern Hills in September 1921.

Published by
REARDON PUBLISHING
PO Box 919, Cheltenham, Glos, GL50 9AN.
Email: reardon@bigfoot.com

Copyright © 2014

Words and Walk Photographs by Frank Partridge

ISBN: 9781874192862

Cover images and
Gustav Holst illustrations by Paul Taylor

Book Design by Nicholas Reardon

Acknowledgements

Our thanks to the following individuals and organisations for their help in
creating the walk and guidebook:

Trustees and volunteers at the Holst Birthplace Museum; Steve Blake;
Steve Brook; Susanne Grün; Vanessa Zecha; the Long Distance Walkers
Association; openstreetmap.org; the Ramblers Association;
Gloucestershire County Council Highways Department;
Friends of Pittville.

GUSTAV HOLST WAY

Foreword

The Gustav Holst Way is a medium distance rambler's route from Cranham to Wyck Rissington, via Cheltenham and Bourton-on-the-Water. Each place has close associations with the composer, and the broad stretch of Cotswold country that connects these important milestones in Holst's life and musical career was well known to him. He recorded many a pleasant day spent walking in the hills. Towards the end of his life, when the composer was too sickly and frail to negotiate the undulating terrain on foot, he took a joyous, leisurely motoring tour of the Cotswolds, accompanied by his brother Emil – by then a Hollywood actor – and his daughter Imogen. We like to think that on this final family excursion they visited many of Gustav's old haunts along the way between Cranham and Wyck Rissington.

The walk is 35 miles in all (with the four optional detours adding a further eight miles or so) and can be undertaken in either direction. Although the record time for completing the route was set east-to-west from Wyck Rissington to Cranham,[1] the more logical starting point is at Cranham, which played an important part in Holst's childhood, with the natural conclusion at Wyck Rissington, where his professional music career began. It is the west-to-east route that is described in this guidebook.

For the convenience of walkers, the route is divided into five sections, ranging in length from about 6-8 miles. The sections are graded for difficulty according to the classification system used by the Ramblers Association and estimated times are given at the start of each section. Walking times can vary considerably depending on the weather, the time of year, the underfoot conditions and the walker's level of fitness. Convenient access points, parking and refreshment stops can be found in the appendix. Special points of interest and historical notes appear in shaded boxes at the end of each section.

Gustav Holst Way: Ups and Downs

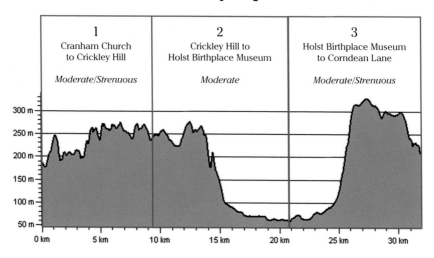

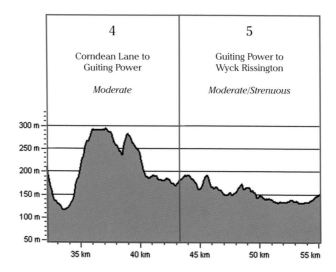

Two of the Ramblers Association's five walk categories apply to the Gustav Holst Way. 'Moderate' is suitable for people with some experience of country walking and a reasonable level of fitness. It may include some steep paths and open country. Walking boots and warm, waterproof clothing are recommended. 'Strenuous' is for experienced ramblers with an above average fitness level. This grade of walk may include hills and rough country. Walking boots and warm, waterproof clothing are essential, and when underfoot conditions are wet, an Alpine pole would be useful. 'Moderate/strenuous' is a mixture of the two.

Author's Note

In writing the first guidebook to the Gustav Holst Way, published exactly 100 years after the young composer began work on *The Planets*, I am indebted to the dedicated groundwork of several members of the Holst Birthplace Trust who helped bring the walk into being. The route was originally conceived by former Trustee Brian Carvell, who wanted to create a permanent memorial to Gustav Holst's life-long connection with this glorious corner of England. A committee was formed under the chairmanship of Roger Graham to develop the plan, scope out the route and secure roundels and signposts at key points.

While they walked the route volunteers took notes and compiled the first written guide, which formed the prototype of this book. By 2011 their work was done, and the walk was officially opened with a ceremony at the Holst Birthplace Museum in Cheltenham in May of that year.

This guidebook remains faithful to the original route, and its division into five easily walkable sections, despite the mild temptation to create seven sections, not five, and name each of them after one of Holst's planets. I can vouch that there are stretches of this sometimes challenging trek which cry out to be described as *Mars, the Bringer of War* or *Saturn, The Bringer of Old Age.*

The one planet Holst left out of his masterpiece was Earth itself. Might I suggest that the Gustav Holst Way completes the set for the composer, by guiding you through some of the loveliest acres to be found anywhere on his 'missing' planet?

The bulk of my own research took place during a mercifully fine and dry August, when I was accompanied by Sara Salvidge from the Holst Birthplace Museum in Cheltenham. Sara's sense of direction is almost as unreliable as mine and, through no fault of the team who laid out the route and roundels, we lost our way on numerous occasions. In retrospect, it might have helped if we had thought to bring a map with us. My thanks to Sara for her extensive local knowledge and calm, unflustered demeanour whenever we strayed from the straight and narrow, and to the volunteers who kindly drove deep into the Cotswolds to collect us when each day's walking was done.

Now, for the first time, we present everything you need to complete the Gustav Holst Way at whatever pace you prefer: an illustrated description of the route and all its major features, alongside a series of clear and simple maps illustrating each of the five sections. The bracketed numerals dotted throughout the text correspond with important points on the maps, to help with orientation. You never know, but if Sara and I attempt the walk again and remember to take this guidebook with us, we might manage to keep on the right track next time.

Frank Partridge

The Gustav Holst Way

Sections   Page

1   Cranham Church to Crickley Hill (5.7 miles/ 9.2 km)   9

2   Crickley Hill to Holst Birthplace Museum (7.3 miles/11.5km)   15

3   Holst Birthplace Museum to Corndean Lane (7 miles/11.3km) 29

4   Corndean Lane to Guiting Power (6.9 miles/11.1km)   39

5   Guiting Power to Wyck Rissington (8.15 miles/13.1km)   47

Detours

1   All Saints Church, Cheltenham (1.3 miles/2.1 km)   23

2   Cleeve Hill and the Cotswold Way (3.8 miles/6.1 km)   35

3   Spoonley Wood and the Roman villa (1.2 miles/1.9 km)   42

4   Naunton village (1.5 miles/2.4 km)   49

Appendix   61

---

[1] *The Record-Setter*

On 14 April 2011, seventeen-year-old Will Wood left Wyck Rissington church at 6:25am and arrived at Cranham church at 7:40pm: his time of 13 hours 15 minutes is the fastest recorded walk/run along the length of the Gustav Holst Way. Will was being sponsored to enable him to travel to Zambia, where he helped build a shelter for elderly people whose families had died of AIDS. He chose the Holst Way after being inspired by the composer's work. Shortly before his record-setting exploits he had played the oboe with the Gloucestershire Youth Orchestra in a performance of The Planets *at Tewkesbury Abbey.*

Section 1

Cranham Church to Crickley Hill

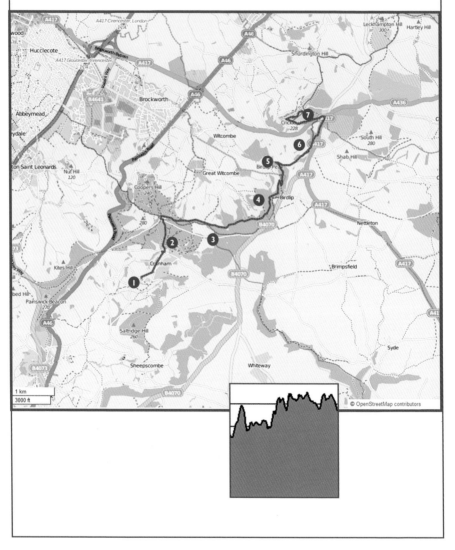

Section 1
Cranham Church (grid ref 891124) to Crickley Hill

Distance: 5.7 miles/9.2 km
Grading: Moderate/strenuous
Time: 3 hours

From lofty Cranham village through extensive beech woods to pass along the Cotswold Edge, emerging on open, high ground with magnificent views, ending at Crickley Hill Country Park.

The starting point of the Gustav Holst Way is the 14th century church of St James the Great (1) on the south-west side of Cranham: a place of fond family memories for the budding composer. Holst's mother Clara played the harmonium and arranged the flowers at the church, and her highly musical son would surely have taken to the keyboard on some of his regular visits. Set on an escarpment on a western fold of the Cotswolds, Cranham is almost completely encircled by ancient beech woods. Clinging to the hillside, its upper reaches extend as high as 923ft (281m): the village in midwinter can be bleak indeed, and if you plan to tackle this opening section any time between November and March, you would be wise to check the local weather forecast before setting off.

*St James the Great Church
Cranham*

In common with many churches in the area, St James boasts a colourful array of kneelers embroidered by the parishioners, one of which is dedicated to Holst's hymn and embellished with snowflakes and a musical notation of his melody. The church briefly found itself in the glare of the media in the summer of 2011, when the pop star Lily Allen was married there.

Outside the church, a distinctive green roundel on the noticeboard indicates the 'official' start of the Holst Way. The composer's bespectacled silhouette on posts (and stickers on lamp-posts) will be your constant companion over the next 35 miles.

Follow the road until you pass the primary school on the right. To the left, a gently sloping sward of grass leads you downhill to a track and a wooden swing-gate giving access to Cranham Common. A little further on is the ivy-covered Black Horse Inn.

Turn left at the pub, dropping towards the lower part of the village. After 80m you pass Midwinter Cottage (2), its name marked on a white wrought-iron gate.

Continue downhill to the lower part of the village and turn right onto the main street. Walk about 50m uphill and turn left onto the signposted footpath, which crosses a stream and enters Buckholt Wood. A wider path intersects with this path, but continue straight ahead on a gradually steepening gradient. Yellow directional arrows marked on tree trunks point the way up the wooded slope, which can be exceptionally muddy in wet conditions. Keep going for about 400m until you arrive at a T-junction. Turn left, and scramble up the steeper and narrower path that eventually emerges from the wood at a road, opposite Woodland House. Buckholt Wood is one of two or three sections of the walk where you can easily lose your way. If this happens, keep going up the slope and regain your bearings at the road.

Cross the road at Woodland House and turn left, passing a larger property called 'The Buckholt' (3). This house has close associations with the Holst family *(see page 12)*. At the end of the garden wall, turn right off the road and take the right of two signed footpaths. After 150m, turn right onto a forest track which makes a gentle descent through the trees until it meets the Cotswold Way, the 102-mile National Trail between Bath Abbey and Chipping Campden. Turn right onto this much wider, well-marked path which follows the line of the Cotswold edge as it passes through Witcombe Wood. Shortly after a left turn at a T-junction (clearly marked by roundels) the path crosses the road just below Birdlip village (4) and continues uphill through the trees for about 400m. At another T-junction, a fingerpost indicates the continuation of the route to the right, but a 200m diversion left to 'The Peak' (5) will be rewarded with panoramic views over the scarp edge to the Severn Vale. Make sure you keep to the left (of several paths) on your return to the fingerpost.

From here, the Holst/Cotswold Way zig-zags as it nears the edge of the wood and takes a left turn through a gate into an open field: welcome daylight after the best part of an hour's walking beneath the shady canopy of beech trees. Keep to the left of the field, pass through another gate, and turn right up a flight of steps shortly after a solitary white house appears in the distance. A little further on is the Barrow Wake viewpoint (6), from where the Malvern Hills are usually visible about 20 miles away. Shortly afterwards, the path runs alongside the A417, dropping down towards the Air Balloon public house beside a very busy roundabout. On the far side, pass through a gate into some open National Trust land signposted 'The Scrubs' that is part of Crickley Hill Country Park, a Site of Special Scientific Interest (SSSI) containing an Iron Age hill-fort and other, earlier, ancient settlements dating from 3500BC and finally abandoned during the Dark Ages, around 500AD. Follow the Cotswold Way signs through the park to the visitor centre (7), which has some interesting displays explaining the development of the site, toilets, and offers a limited selection of snacks and refreshments between 1 April and 30 September.

When did the Great War end?

The gateway to Cranham church was built in thanksgiving for victory in the Great War. Dated 1914-19, it commemorates 'seven of Cranham and five of Prinknash' who died in the conflict. Why 1919? Although an Armistice was agreed between the Allies and Germany in November 1918, peace was not officially declared between Britain and Germany until the Treaty of Versailles the following June, and it was as late as September 1919 before a peace accord was finally agreed between the Allies and Austria. Many Great War memorials around the country (including the one on the Promenade in Cheltenham) reflect this lengthy delay in bringing 'the war to end all wars' to a conclusion.

Midwinter Cottage

While staying at the cottage in 1904, Holst composed a setting for 'In the Bleak Midwinter' to a poem by Christina Rossetti that had been published 32 years earlier. Christina was the sister and muse of the Pre-Raphaelite Brotherhood leader, Dante Gabriel Rossetti. She knew Gloucestershire well, often visiting her uncle, Henry Polydore, who lived in Cheltenham. The hymn, known as Cranham, first appeared in the English Hymnal of 1906 and, although other composers (including Benjamin Britten and Harold Edwin Darke) have put Rossetti's words to music, Holst's plaintive melody remains among the most evocative of all English Christmas carols.

The Buckholt

Much extended over the years, this house was originally known as Buckholt Cottage and belonged to Holst's maternal great-grandfather, David Whatley, whose daughter Mary was born in 1806. Mary married Samuel Lediard at the age of 20, and one of their nine children was Clara, Holst's mother. After her husband died suddenly of typhoid fever in 1852, Mary had to look after the large family alone, and lived with them in Buckholt Cottage for some years before moving to No 4 Pittville Terrace in Cheltenham to enable her to send Clara to Cheltenham Ladies' College, and her son Henry to Cheltenham College. Clara married Adolphus von Holst, and their son Gustav was born in the house in 1874. Grandmother Mary ended her days at Cowley, near Oxford, where she died in 1895.

The Devil's Chimney

Section 2

Crickley Hill to Holst Birthplace Museum

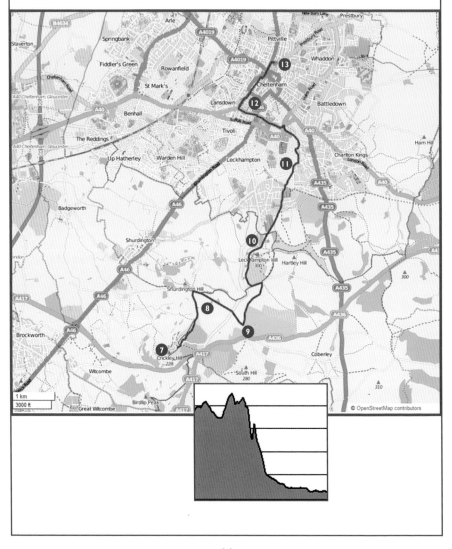

Section 2
Crickley Hill (grid ref 930164)
to Holst Birthplace Museum

Distance: 7.3 miles/11.5km
Grading: Moderate
Time: 3 hours

From Crickley Hill country park along the Cotswold Edge to Leckhampton Hill, passing Devil's Chimney before descending on an old quarry incline to Cheltenham and finishing at Holst's birthplace in Pittville.

Turning right out of the Crickley Hill visitor centre **(7)**, join the Cotswold Way. After 100m, turn left through a gap in the fence and immediately right through a gate. After the best part of a mile turn right into Greenway Lane, which is bordered by beech trees (some more than 250 years old) and leads to a crossroads. Carry straight on along a minor road which passes the National Star College **(8)** to the right.

Continue along the lane for approximately 200m, and turn left on to a track signposted 'Cotswold Way, Leckhampton Hill 1½ miles, Restricted Byway'. The track makes a steady ascent past Cotswold Hills Golf Club, skirting a large field to reach a T-junction at Hartley Lane **(9)**. Turn left and follow the lane for 300m before turning right at the Cotswold Way sign on to a narrow track which climbs through trees and shrubs above Wagoner's Quarry car park on the left, leading to a swathe of open grassland on the edge of the escarpment. Much of the stone removed from the disused quarry was used for the remarkable transformation of Cheltenham from provincial backwater to fashionable spa resort in Regency times. In most weathers, the views from Leckhampton Hill to the north and west are arresting, with the town spread out across the foreground and the distinctive outline of the Malvern and Welsh Hills in the distance.

About 400m further on, leave the Cotswold Way to follow a signed path which drops down the hill to the left to provide another memorable view - of the legendary Devil's Chimney **(10)** (grid ref 946184), one of the major landmarks of the walk (*see pp 13 & 24*).

15

Leckhampton Hill and view from the Devil's Chimney

From here, the trail descends the once rich stone-quarrying slopes of Leckhampton Hill. Continue along the escarpment until a stony path drops quite sharply past old quarry buildings on the right to reach Daisy Bank Road. When underfoot conditions are slippery, a stick or an Alpine pole would be a useful accessory here. There is a car park about 200m down the road on the left.

A short distance beyond the car park on Daisy Bank Road is a modest-looking house, Tramway Cottage, that merits a significant footnote in English social history *(see pp 24-25).*

Crossing Daisy Bank Road, continue over a metal stile down some steps on the far side, then more steeply down to the right before it levels out in a wooded section and emerges on a stretch of open common. The path is not marked here, but the masts on top of Cleeve Hill *(below)* about four miles away are a useful aiming point.

Soon the trail reaches another patch of woodland. There are no roundels to assist orientation here, so be sure to enter the left edge of the wood and fork left when the path divides immediately afterwards. Whatever the weather conditions, this is one of the muddiest sections of the walk, but after a slippery ten-minute slog you emerge to the left of a housing estate and enter the outskirts of Cheltenham. A Holst Way sticker on a metal Public Footpath sign soon confirms your bearings. Pass behind some houses to reach Southfield Approach. Cross the road by the roundel to walk along the edge of the Old Patesians' playing field, past an attractive children's playground and the clubhouse, until you come to a gate on the left leading to a footbridge across an old railway cutting of the Cheltenham to Banbury line (a casualty of Dr Beeching's dismantling of Britain's rural railway network in the early 1960s.) Keep going in the same direction along Greatfield Drive. As the road curves to the right, follow the green Public Footpath sign (with a small Holst roundel sticker) that leads you, diagonally, to the left of the houses before reaching a mini roundabout where three roads converge. Continue straight ahead along Moorend Road.

After about 300m, look out for some railings on the left, and follow a cycleway/footpath leading to the town centre. The path winds through a housing estate, passing a duckpond on the right, to reach a wide open space called Cox's Meadow (11). Look out for a clump of six young oak trees to the right. These were planted by the Cheltenham Tree Group in June 2012 to celebrate the Queen's diamond jubilee, with cuttings taken from an oak planted by the then Princess Elizabeth on her visit to Cheltenham 61 years earlier. At first sight, Cox's Meadow appears to be a purely recreational area, but its main purpose is to act as a water storage system to protect Cheltenham from flooding. (Unfortunately, this failed to prevent the area being overwhelmed by catastrophic floods in the summer of 2007.)

The cycleway and path continue straight ahead to reach the A40 Old Bath Road. Cross the road at the pedestrian light, turn left and then immediately right into Sandford Road. You are now entering the historic part of Cheltenham. Pass the General Hospital, and then Cheltenham College. At the end of Sandford Road, the traffic lights form a staggered junction. Turn right and immediately left into Montpellier Terrace, past the birthplace (No 91, with an inscription on the wall) of the artist, naturalist and explorer Dr Edward Wilson, who was a member of both Captain Scott's Antarctic expeditions and died alongside him on their return from the South Pole in 1912, only eleven miles from the food depot that would have saved them.

Holst was naturally right-handed, but held the baton in his left hand because of the acute neuritis he suffered in his right.

Wilson is commemorated in a display panel in the College grounds by the traffic lights.

You have now reached the celebrated Montpellier district of Cheltenham, laid out with attractive villas and terraces surrounding ornamental gardens. Its name was derived from the spa town in southern France, and the *chichi* shops, cafés and intimate, shady courtyards of Cheltenham's Montpellier have a distinctly continental flavour. Most eye-catching of all is Montpellier Walk, reached by turning right at the roundabout at the end of Montpellier Terrace. Apart from visiting the most interesting shopping street in Cheltenham, another good reason for lingering here is the Montpellier Rotunda *(see p. 25)* directly across the road.

Continue along Montpellier Walk towards the town centre, admiring the smart shops and cafés, the pretty courtyards and the shopfronts adorned with 32 caryatids that might have been 'borrowed' from the Acropolis itself. Just after passing the Queen's Hotel on the right, bear right into the Promenade, bordering the flower-filled Imperial Gardens. Halfway along the gardens, set back a little from the pavement, is a fountain with a fine bronze statue of Gustav Holst **(12)**, brandishing a conductor's baton in his left hand, with seven plaques depicting the Planets incorporated into the plinth. Designed by Anthony Stones, the fountain was unveiled in 2008, largely funded by a bequest from Elizabeth Hamond, a long-time Cheltenham resident who was devoted to the town.

In Holst's day the broad, tree-lined Promenade was a residential street where his father's pupils gave concerts. Today it is a handsome mix of offices, municipal buildings and shops, with a strip of green running along the western side (to the left) containing floral displays, the notable Neptune Fountain, a statue of the explorer Edward Wilson and a Great War memorial (like Cranham's, dating the conflict 1914-19.) After a pedestrianised section, the Promenade reaches the High Street, the original axis of the town, but now a shoddily redeveloped shadow of its former self. Among the absentees in this modern mish-mash are the original building of Pate's Grammar School, which Holst attended, and the Corn Exchange, which staged the first full performance of *Lansdown Castle* in February 1893, with Holst himself on piano. The critical reception was mixed, ranging from "a slender stringing together of various incidents more or less improbable" to "giving evidence not only of genius but also of careful and laborious study". One of the infuriating beauties of the performing arts is that no two people can ever agree about it.

The Neptune Fountain

At the High Street, turn right and immediately left into Pittville Street. After crossing Albion Street this becomes Portland Street. Keep straight on, past the Masonic Hall on the left and then Holy Trinity Church on the right. Immediately beyond the church an alleyway leads off the pavement on Portland Street behind Clarence Road. At the entrance to the alleyway two iron posts mark the southern boundary of the Pittville Estate, established in 1824 by a wealthy landowner, Joseph Pitt *(see page 26).*

The house where Gustav Holst was born was built as part of the estate in 1832. At the top of Portland Street, turn right at the traffic lights into Clarence Road and arrive at No 4, the Holst Birthplace Museum **(13).**

Holst Birthplace Museum

Detour 1: All Saints Church

After visiting the Museum, turn right at the bottom of the steps and cross Clarence Road just before the junction. The ornamental gates (*see page 35*) directly ahead formed the original entrance to Pittville Park, but now lead into Pittville Lawn, an attractive residential street. After about 200m turn right (at Wellington Road) and continue for another 200m before taking the third exit of a five-point roundabout into Pittville Circus. Cross the centre of the Circus and continue down Pittville Circus Road for 150m before bearing right at a mini roundabout into All Saints Road. Proceed with care at each of these busy junctions because there are no pedestrian crossings. All Saints Church is a short distance down the road on the left.

Established in 1868, this striking, Grade 1 listed church is the place of worship most closely associated with Gustav Holst. His parents, Adolph and Clara, were married here in 1871; Adolph was an organist and choirmaster at the church for 25 years. Holst himself was baptised there, sang in the choir and played the violin and trombone in small orchestras brought together for special occasions. Son followed father by taking his turn at the organ, on which it is likely that he composed his *Four Voluntaries for Organ* in 1891. Holst's *Duet for Trombone and Organ*, composed in 1894 and first performed a year later, was played at All Saints in September 2012 in a concert that reunited Holst's restored trombone and the church organ for the first time in more than a century.

Some of the notable stained glass in All Saints was designed by Edward Coley Burne-Jones (1833-98), a leading light of the later pre-Raphaelite movement.

Retrace your steps as far as Pittville Park for the continuation of the Holst Way on page 28.

Retrace your steps as far as Pittville Park for the continuation of the Holst Way on page 28.

National Star College

The National Star College is an independent specialist college for students who have physical, sensory or learning disabilities. Their studies, and the qualifications they achieve, enable them to gain real life work experience. The original building used by the college was Ullenwood Manor, built in 1857. In recent years the complex has been extensively developed, and its restaurant, the Star Bistro, gained national fame in 2013 when it was voted runner-up in the ITV series *Food, Glorious Food*. The bistro sources all its fresh food locally.

The Devil's Chimney

This craggy finger of rock projecting from a terrace on the scarp face is almost certainly the work of 18th century quarrymen, who fashioned a block of limestone to appear a good deal more dramatic than nature intended. The legend of the pinnacle, which survived an earthquake in 1926, is more colourful. Provoked by the many churches in the vicinity, the Devil sat on top of Leckhampton Hill and hurled stones at churchgoers. They threw the stones back, drove him underground and trapped him there. For years the public had access to the pinnacle, and various hair-raising climbing stunts took place there. It is said that as many as 13 people once managed to perch on the top at the same time, but a combination of erosion and Health and Safety legislation put paid to such capers, and the chimney has been securely fenced off since 1985 – but it still makes for a memorable picture.

Tramway Cottage and the Leckhampton Riots

A short distance beyond the car park on Daisy Bank Road is a modest-looking house, Tramway Cottage, that merits a significant footnote in English social history. The site was the focus of a violent dispute in the early 20th century, when local people risked their liberty to preserve their right to roam over Leckhampton Hill, a popular haunt of families enjoying an afternoon out and a short-cut for children walking to school from the outlying villages. When the Leckhampton Estate sold the land to businessman Henry J. Dale in 1894 the new owner fenced off more than twenty acres in an attempt to restrict public access, and built Tramway Cottage for the quarry foreman over a footpath that crossed Daisy Bank Road. In July 1902 a group of men known as the Leckhampton Stalwarts, supported by 10,000 protestors, took the law into their hands, tore down fencing and destroyed the cottage. They were arrested, but no charges were brought. Dale rebuilt the cottage and, although negotiations continued for some years, they proved fruitless. Finally, on Good Friday 1906, the normally happy Easter celebrations on the hill turned ugly, and protestors once again descended on the cottage. Fencing was knocked down, but the police arrived before they could do any further damage. This time the ringleaders were arrested and imprisoned, but the public right of way was preserved in perpetuity.

Holst at the Rotunda

The Rotunda started life as a Pump Room, and some of Gustav Holst's early works were performed there. In late 1891, two afternoon concerts featured his *Scherzo* and *Intermezzo*, the latter earning his first glowing newspaper review: 'The work was well received and the youthful composer bowed his acknowledgements.' Holst returned to the Rotunda in December 1892 to conduct parts of his operetta *Lansdown Castle*.

The Rotunda's skylit dome and central chandelier have been well preserved, but even in Holst's time the building was not what it was originally intended to be. A decade before those historic performances it had been bought by the Worcester City and County Bank, who allowed occasional balls and concerts to be staged - presumably after cashing-up time.

Holst at Cheltenham Town Hall

The prominent building at the north-east corner of Imperial Gardens is the Baroque-style Town Hall, which opened in December 1903. The main hall has been Cheltenham's principal music venue ever since, with seating for about 1,000. It was here that Holst attended two concerts in March 1927 as part of a festival given in his honour. At the first event he was given a civic welcome and conducted his *Somerset Rhapsody* and *The Planets*. During the interval he made a speech saying that all the kindness he had received made him feel more of a citizen of Cheltenham than ever before. Afterwards he deemed the occasion the "most overwhelming event" of his life, and in return promised the town the first English performance of *Egdon Heath*, which he duly conducted at the Town Hall in February 1928.

The rear of the Town Hall viewed from the Holst Statue

Pittville

Pittville was Joseph Pitt's *grand projet*: a new town on the northern outskirts of Cheltenham, embracing a spa, ornamental gardens and lakes, miles of gravelled walks and rides, an exclusive residential area of more than 500 villas and terraces, and a new church. By 1833, when the Scottish writer Catherine Sinclair visited Pittville, the scheme was well advanced. She described in her diary '... a scene of gorgeous magnificence ... sprinkled with houses of every size, shape and character – Grecian temples, Italian villas and citizen's boxes, so fresh and clear you would imagine they were all blown out at once like soap bubbles.' A national banking crisis and other misfortunes eventually led to Pitt's financial ruin, but much of his blueprint survives today, as we can see on the next stage of the walk, and Pittville remains one of Cheltenham's jewels.

Holst's Birthplace

Gustav Holst was born at 4 Pittville Terrace (later renamed as 4 Clarence Road) on 21 September 1874 and lived there throughout his early childhood. The damp, terraced house where he composed music for the first time probably exacerbated his neuritis and asthma, putting extra strain on his weak heart. But it also instilled in him a fierce determination to improve the lot of the under-privileged. On the advice of his doctor, the weak and anaemic boy took up walking, and rarely missed an opportunity to explore the Cotswolds, in all weathers. He is said to have habitually carried a train timetable in one pocket and a bus timetable in the other. Holst's mother, Clara, died in February 1882 (when he was seven) and the family moved to No 1 Vittoria Walk. This house has now been demolished. In the spring of 1891 they moved again, to apartments at 46 Lansdown Crescent, from where Holst went to study at the Royal College of Music in London.

In 1949 a commemorative plaque was unveiled at the house in Clarence Road by Holst's friend and fellow composer Vaughan Williams. The Holst Birthplace Museum was established in his centenary year of 1974, with considerable help from his daughter, Imogen, who donated a number of the items to be seen in the museum today. The museum opened to the public in 1975 and was managed by Cheltenham Borough Council until 2000, when the independent Holst Birthplace Trust took over.

Section 3

Holst Birthplace Museum to Corndean Lane

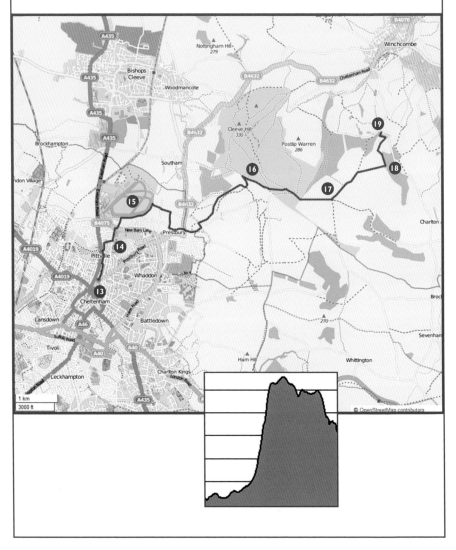

Section 3
Holst Birthplace Museum (grid ref 935228) to Corndean Lane

Distance: 7 miles/11.3km
Grading: Moderate/strenuous
Time: 3 hours

From Cheltenham to the north Cotswolds via the racecourse and Prestbury village; climb to the open common of Cleeve Hill; pass Belas Knap long barrow before descending through woods to rural Corndean Lane.

Turn right out of the Holst Birthplace Museum and cross Clarence Road near the junction. Straight ahead are the Pittville Gates, leading into leafy Pittville Lawn, with its fine early 19th century houses.

Pittville Gates

Follow Pittville Lawn and cross Wellington Road into Pittville Park. Walk through the park for about half a mile as far as the lake, which can be skirted in either direction. Carry on up the grassy slope to the green-domed

Pittville Pump Room

The Pittville Pump

Pittville Pump Room (14), surrounded on three sides by a stately colonnade of ionic columns: one of the most striking examples of Regency architecture in Cheltenham.

Leave the Pump Room by the road to the right – East Approach Drive – where you catch an early glimpse of the Cotswold Edge on the skyline straight ahead. Later today, or next time you tackle the walk, you're going to have to climb it!

At the end of the road turn left into Albert Road. Continue for about 350m to the mini roundabout, cross the road, turn right and take the public footpath to the left about 40m from the junction. Follow this track between houses and through a kissing gate to enter the grounds of Cheltenham Racecourse (15).

Pick up the perimeter path going off to the right, keeping the racecourse on your left. Towards the top of a small incline take the footpath (marked Cheltenham Circular Path) to the right towards a stile. Cross the stile, walk along Park Lane and by the post box cross the road diagonally to enter Shaw Green Lane. This is the village of Prestbury, with its pleasing mix of old and new houses, but widely held to be one of the most haunted villages in Britain. Superstitious walkers will be relieved to know that the Holst Way proceeds at a safe distance from almost all of the reputedly haunted sites.

About 200m along Shaw Green Lane, take a footpath to the right between the houses, marked 'Cheltenham Circular Path', and continue across a field towards the church until you come to a road. Turn left along Mill Street past The Plough pub, cross a busy main road and continue straight ahead up Mill Lane. After 300m make a left turn at the crossroads into Queenwood Grove. The road curves round to the right in the direction of Cleeve Hill, with its three large radio masts at the summit. Ignore two footpath signs (one on either side) and take the third one, to the left, near the end of the tarmac beside a house named Highcroft.

Follow this path over a stile into a field and climb the hill on a steadily steepening gradient, bearing right to make the tricky manoeuvre of crossing a stone stile, before passing a small orchard of fir trees on the right. The path continues uphill, crossing another stile - easier to negotiate than the last - into fields alongside Queens Wood, which is spectacularly carpeted by bluebells in the spring. Keeping a steady bearing, cross two fields and three more stiles before turning right towards a small meadow, reached by crossing yet another stile. The meadow, known as Wheeler's, is a Site of Special Scientific Interest (SSSI) because of its wild flowers, notably several species of orchids and cowslips in season. The going hereabouts is tough because there is little relief on the ascent, but as you gain height wonderful views of Cheltenham open up behind you.

After leaving the meadow, it's easy to lose the Holst Way path as it converges with several others, including the Cotswold Way. At the point where the path reaches a four-way junction, at the base of a series of grassy mounds, bear left on a stony path up the hill; take a sharp left and continue the ascent on a broader path, leading to the gate to Cleeve Common (16). Go through the gate and locate the Holst Way roundel on the right, pointing you in the direction of the radio masts. Turn sharply right and head directly towards the masts, keeping a weather-beaten dry stone wall on your right. (If you lose your way on this somewhat confusing section, take any route uphill to the plateau at the top, using the radio masts as your target, and pick up the Holst Way again on Cleeve Common.)

At 1,083ft (330m) above sea level, Cleeve Common is the highest point in the Cotswolds: from here the Malvern Hills and the Black Mountains in Wales are clearly visible in all but misty weather. The Common is the last remaining area of unenclosed wasteland in the Cotswolds, criss-crossed by numerous paths and bridleways and sprinkled with a prodigious number of wild flowers: five species of orchid grow near the perimeter, but the main attraction for non-botanists is the feeling of tramping over a stretch of timeless, unspoilt wilderness – and the unsurpassed views.

Just after passing the masts, turn left towards some circular fencing about 150m ahead, which surrounds a dew pond, well restored by local volunteer wardens. Continue past the pond until you see a broader path coming in from the left. Turn right at a fence post bearing both Holst Way and Winchcombe Way roundels, pass between some gorse bushes and make for the edge of the common. There you go through a metal gate, where the Holst Way roundel is one of a competing group of four. The breezy common, cleared for grazing in prehistoric times and conveying a feeling of being on top of the world, is understandably a magnet for every Cotswold rambler, as well as kite-flyers and model aircraft enthusiasts.

Now you begin a welcome descent. Follow the path between two fields and through a copse to the remains of Wontley Farm buildings **(17)**, where you turn left into a farm track, its hedgerows thick with wild flowers in summer, and home to nesting thrushes.

Wontley Farm buildings

A quarter of a mile further on the new route of the Cotswold Way joins from the left. A similar distance beyond that, turn right on the Cotswold Way towards the distinctive low mound of Belas Knap **(18),** which lies straight ahead at the end of the field *(see p. 37)*.

Leaving Belas Knap via some stone steps, turn left through a kissing gate along the edge of the wood (still following the Cotswold Way.) To the right there are glimpses of Sudeley Castle and the small town of Winchcombe in the valley below, and the Malvern Hills on the horizon directly ahead. Turn right down a sharply sloping field; turn left at the bottom of the slope and then right into another belt of woodland. A stile with a Holst Way roundel leads on to Corndean Lane **(19)** and the end of the third section of the walk. (Winchcombe, with its buses, refreshments and B&Bs, is about a mile down the hill to the left.)

Detour 2: Cleeve Hill loop

If you want to prolong the enjoyment of this breathtaking section of the Holst Way, the well-trodden Cleeve Hill Loop adds about four miles (two hours) to the walk, rejoining the linear route at Belas Knap. After entering Cleeve Common through the gate, simply carry straight on looking out for the Cotswold Way roundels and waymarks. The views in every direction are among the finest in southern England, with a sweeping panorama encompassing the Forest of Dean, the Severn Vale, the Malverns, Black Mountains and Brecon Beacons. The landscape is carpeted with wild flowers and unusual orchids because it has never been farmed; the protected Roman snail and several species of butterfly can also be seen. There's a handy refreshment stop at the golf clubhouse, which is open to the public.

Pittville Gates

The Pittville Gates, erected in 1833, form a suitably grand entrance to Cheltenham's largest ornamental park. The elaborate wrought-iron 'overthrow', with the Borough's coat of arms, was added in 1897 in time for a visit by the Prince of Wales during Queen Victoria's Diamond Jubilee year. For more than 130 years, traffic was allowed to pass through the gates, but in 1965 a furniture lorry caught one of the central pillars and brought the arch crashing down. After it was repaired and reinstalled, the council banned through traffic. In 1972, the gates were awarded Grade II status by English Heritage, but both the pillars and metalwork deteriorated badly over time, and in 2011 a local historical group, Friends of Pittville (www.friendsofpittville.org) launched a successful restoration programme to restore the gates and the overthrow to their original condition, and replace the stone piers.

Pittville Pump Room

This impressive pile was designed by a local architect, John Forbes, and built between 1825 and 1830 at the height of Cheltenham's fame as a spa resort. Costing upwards of £40,000 to build – at the time, an eye-watering sum - the Pump Room was modelled on the Greek temple of Illissus in Athens. The figures on the parapet above the colonnade represent Hygeia, the Greek goddess of health, holding a serpent drinking from a saucer; her father, Aesculapius, also holding a serpent and a large staff; and the physician, Hippocrates. The original sculptures were erected in 1827; the figures we see today are copies installed in 1965.

The waters had been discovered around 1716 on a site now occupied by Cheltenham Ladies' College, and received royal approval in 1788 when George III and Queen Charlotte visited the spa for five weeks. In the 20th century the building fell into decline, ravaged by dry rot and knocked about by British and US troops billeted there during World War II. The entrance to the Pump Room is on the right-hand side of the building. The interior is dominated by the chandeliered great hall, surmounted by a gallery and central dome, and now a popular venue for weddings and classical music concerts: the acoustics are stunning. To the right of the hall is the pump, ornamentally set in marble and scagliola, which draws water through a shaft sunk more than 30 metres below ground to the source. Unlike many other English spa waters, Cheltenham's is alkaline, not 'rotten egg' sulphurous, and pleasant to taste after passing through Health and Safety-approved filters. Originally, the pump was operated by hand, but electricity does the job today following a major restoration programme in 2005. For some years the water was transported from the Pump Room to a 'Central Spa' in Cheltenham Town Hall, in order to make it available to residents and visitors in a more convenient location, but the secondary spa is no longer used, and the Pump Room is the only place where Cheltenham spa water can be drunk directly from the source. The venue is open between 10am-4pm from Wednesday to Sunday, except when private functions are being held.

Cheltenham Racecourse

Horse racing, gambling and Cheltenham have been closely associated for nearly two centuries, but the undulating course that lies in a natural amphitheatre at the foot of Cleeve Hill is not where the sport originated in the area. There was once a track, grandstand and space for up to 50,000 spectators on Cleeve Hill itself, and a Gold Cup race took place there in its second year, 1819. A decade later, the Anglican Rector of Cheltenham decided to take action against the pickpockets, drunkards and other low life who frequented the meetings, and whipped up such indignation amongst his parishioners that they hurled rocks and bottles at the horses and jockeys, and during the off-season burnt the course facilities to the ground. Racing moved to Prestbury Park for a few years, but fell into decline until it was re-established at its present venue in 1898. The first National Hunt festival was held in 1911, and the sport produced its first household name when Golden Miller won the Gold Cup five times in the 1930s.

From 1912 until 1976, the racecourse had its own railway station connected to the national network, and both steam and diesel trains returned there in 2003 following restoration by volunteers from the Gloucestershire Warwickshire Railway. Hundreds of racegoers travel eight miles to the course from the network connection at Toddington. The station building, fringed by Corsican pines, has been well restored, and has toilets and refreshment facilities as well as a large free car park.

Racecourse viewed from Cleeve Hill

Belas Knap (grid ref 021254)

This Neolithic long barrow, measuring nearly 180ft lengthways and dating from around 3000BC, contains four burial chambers and a false entrance at its north end, blocked by a large stone, possibly designed to deter grave-robbers. The real entry points, at the side, would have been invisible when they were closed off and covered with earth. Excavated several times between the 1860s and 1963, Belas Knap has yielded the skeletal remains of 38 men, women and children, as well as animal bones, flint tools and pottery. Belas Knap is one of the most intriguing and iconic sites in the Cotswolds, and an excellent place to pause and soak up the past. The free-to-enter site is well maintained by English Heritage.

Section 4

Corndean Lane to Guiting Power

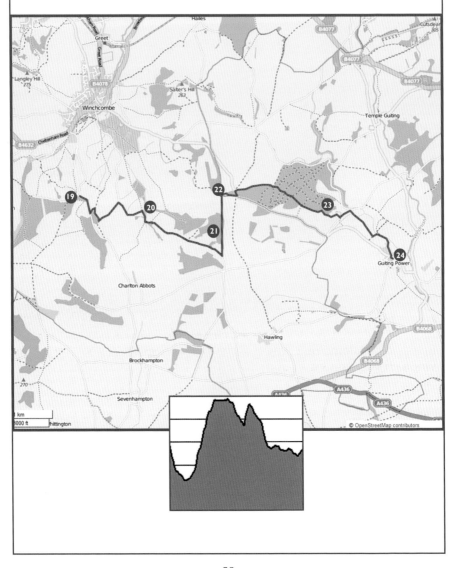

Section 4
Corndean Lane (grid ref 020262) to Guiting Power

Distance: 6.9 miles/11.1km
Grading: Moderate
Time: 3 hours

The scenic highlight of the route, descending into the valley behind Sudeley Castle, climbing to the ancient ridgeway route of the Salt Way, passing commercial forestry and sweeping parkland to finish at the picture-postcard village of Guiting Power.

At Corndean Lane, the Holst Way and Cotswold Way part company, heading off in opposite directions. Our route ascends the attractive wooded lane for about 500m and then takes a sharp left down a track at the side of a wood (marked Private Road Footpath only). After about 100m, take the second turning on the right along a track that passes below Humblebee Cottages and a wood, with open fields and views of Sudeley Castle and Winchcombe on the left. Follow the track over a small rise to a gate - mind your fingers on the metal opening device – before turning left downhill on a grassy track, initially alongside a wire fence. Pass through a second gate and bear left across an open field to reach Newmeadow Farm. The rolling landscape here, with its chequerboard fields punctuated by clumps of trees and hedgerows, is quintessential Cotswold country, and the next few miles are a joy in - almost - all weathers.

At Newmeadow Farm, go through the gate under the trees and turn right along a 'restricted byway'. The track passes a second gate, crosses a small stream and slaloms one way and the other for 400m to join the signed Windrush Way coming in from the left **(20)**.

Follow the track along the valley, curving left as it crosses a stream and then rising slightly beneath trees to arrive at the derelict buildings of Waterhatch.

Just before you reach them, look out for an abandoned but still atmospheric watermill and sluice easily reached along a narrow path through the trees on the right. From Waterhatch, continue uphill along the track for about a mile and a quarter.

Newmeadow Farm

Windrush Way signpost

The steady climb on the uneven surface is taxing on the feet, but there are stretches of smoother tarmac – and the glorious scenery more than atones for any discomfort.

Below lonely but lovely Spoonley Farmhouse three tracks converge: take the middle one, and continue straight uphill. Soon afterwards, you reach a tarmac road. This is the historic Salt Way, part of an ancient ridgeway from the rich salt mines of Droitwich towards the south coast. Pick up the Holst Way again on page 43.

Waterhatch landscape

Spoonley Farmhouse

Detour 3: Spoonley Wood

A fascinating alternative route between Waterhatch and Spoonley Farm – adding about half a mile of heavier going to this section of the walk - passes through Spoonley Wood, which contains foundations of a Roman villa **(21)** excavated in the 19th century. There are no signposts to the villa, and the ramshackle shelter can be hard to spot in summer when the undergrowth is dense. But tracking down this curious, 2,000-year-old piece of history is worth the effort. One of the beauties of this site is that so few people ever go there: you're almost sure to be alone with the stones.

As you leave Waterhatch and reach a signpost with a Holst Way roundel, take a grassy track to the left across a field, keeping to the left of the telegraph wires. At the end of the field, the track becomes a well-defined footpath that bridges a stream and meanders through Spoonley Wood, re-crossing the stream about 400m further on. Shortly after the main path rises and swings to the left, keep a sharp eye open for a subsidiary path leading off to the right, through the scrub to the moss-covered muddle of stones. The most interesting surviving feature of the villa is the tiled floor mosaic, protected from the elements by a corrugated iron roof and plastic

Roman Villa, Spoonley Wood

sheeting weighed down with flat stones. Uncovering the entire floor is an awkward job best left to the specialists, but peel back a corner of the covering to reveal a small section and consider the sophisticated craftsmanship that created it all those years ago.

From the villa, return to the main path, turn right, and climb steadily towards the edge of the wood after negotiating a tricky section that invariably turns to thick, cloying mud in wet conditions. Eventually you emerge on a track. Turn right along the track, which contours across the hillside to rejoin the Holst Way at the junction below Spoonley Farm. Take a sharp left uphill to reach the Salt Way.

Roman mosaic
with protective covering

Back on the Gustav Holst Way, turn left to follow the Salt Way, looking out for both the busy traffic and the superb views towards Winchcombe. Nearly a mile down the road a bridle path comes in from the left: this is the Warden's Way, a long distance footpath that is no longer officially classified. But hereabouts its signs are helpful, because shortly afterwards you turn right to follow it alongside a wall, and then, through a swing gate, past the edge of a wood replete with wild flowers (signed 'Farmcote Estate'), to reach another surfaced lane **(22)**.

Turn left along the lane for a short distance; then turn right to follow the path downhill along the edge of Guiting Wood. The overhanging beech and sycamore trees create a dramatic 'tunnel' effect when in full summer leaf. After two-thirds of a mile you arrive at a four-way junction. Continue straight ahead up a steepish incline into the interior of the shady wood, leaving the Warden's Way in the process. Eventually the path levels off, passing various intersections with forest tracks. Keep straight on, following the waymarked right of way, taking care on some extremely slippery sections. At certain times of the year you will be accompanied by hundreds of scuttling young pheasants beyond the fence, being bred for sport on the adjoining estate. Another 800m further on, when you can see the edge of

Guiting Wood

the wood ahead, leave the rough track (which veers left) and follow a short path leading out of the wood into an open field. Look for a stone marker saying 'No Public Road Here' **(23)**.

Turn left as you leave Guiting Wood, following the perimeter of the trees gently downhill. At the end of the field take a dog-leg right. After 800m, the descent steepens and the path bends left, following a fence towards the buildings of Guiting Manor. When you reach a tarmac drive, turn right and follow it down to a lane. Turn left along the lane, through a gate into an attractive park signposted 'Kineton Public Road'. Soon you reach a crossroads, where there is a car park. Turn right along a track which goes briefly downhill and then across fields for 700m to reach a T-junction in front of a white bungalow. Turn left at the junction and then bend right to follow the track, first downhill through pleasant woodland with a babbling brook for company, and then uphill to emerge at the chocolate-box village of Guiting Power, by the square and the sloping green **(24)**.

Lying on a tributary of the River Windrush, the russet-coloured houses of this horse racing centre cluster around the green, dipping to the village square with its post office cum teashop/bakery that exudes just about everything that was good about Olde England. The village, one of the most photogenic in the Cotswolds, hosts a small but widely renowned music and arts festival every July. In the 19th century it was the home of the Cotswold Stone Pipe factory, some of whose products can still be seen in field walls around the village. Guiting Power boasts two pubs: the forbidding-looking but reassuringly traditional Farmer's Arms, complete with skittle alley, near the village green, and the modernised, racing-themed Hollow Bottom Inn, about 700m along the Winchcombe road. Both are fine places in which to pause and reflect on a glorious, unspoilt corner of the English countryside: probably the most scenic section of the walk. Both pubs have rooms for overnighting walkers.

Section 5

Guiting Power to Wyck Rissington

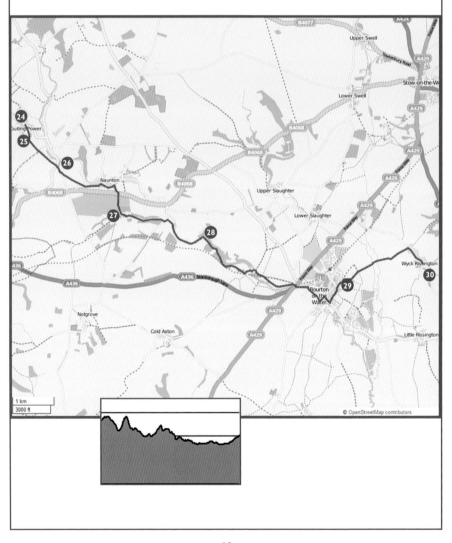

Section 5
Guiting Power (grid ref 095248) to
Wyck Rissington (grid ref 192216)

Distance: 8.15 miles/13.1km
Grading: Moderate/strenuous
Time: 4 hours

From Guiting Power across open fields to the pretty village of Naunton; along the Windrush valley floor to Bourton-on-the-Water; through nature reserves and meadowland to Wyck Rissington.

The fifth and final section of the walk begins at the village green opposite the old post office in Guiting Power (**24**). Take the road that leads to the village hall and St Michael's Church (**25**), sitting on a ridge in splendid isolation.

When you reach the church follow the footpath – part of the Warden's Way again – as it passes between two gates and leads through the churchyard to another gate. Go through and bear left across a large field, aiming for the left hand edge of the farm buildings on the horizon. As you cross the field, look back at the classic Cotswolds tableau you're leaving behind.

Continue towards the end of the field, to where the path descends through a gate and crosses a stream. Now the path narrows as it pushes uphill, but some useful steps assist the climb towards a gate that ushers you in to another large field. Continue until you meet the main road, watching for traffic speeding around the blind bend to the right. Take the lane directly opposite (signposted Naunton 1¼, Stow 6¼), continuing uphill for about 200m before taking a footpath off to the left **(26)**. The well waymarked path soon becomes a farm track that continues to the far edge of a small wood, before crossing a large field with the farm buildings on your right. Leave the field by way of a gate and stile and cross another, grassy field above a valley. Pass through a gate and turn left onto the road that runs down to Naunton village.

Naunton Dovecot

Detour 4: Naunton village

One of the most beautiful villages in the Cotswolds, sleepy Naunton is hidden in a fold of hills formed by the River Windrush on its way to Oxfordshire, where it eventually flows into the Thames. Naunton has many an interesting feature, and a detour through the village is well worthwhile. It boasts the excellent Black Horse pub, but there have been no shops in the village (now something of a dormitory for Cheltenham) since 1999.

After forking left and reaching the bottom of the hill, turn left instead of following the Warden's Way, and 100m further on take the path to the left that leads up to St Andrew's Church. This bright and cheerful place of worship, mainly dating from the 15th century, has two unusual 18th century sundials in the tower, an elaborately carved stone pulpit, and a white Saxon cross set into the wall near the bell chamber. Next to the War Memorial, note the simple wooden cross recovered from the trenches of Flanders and bearing the name of Gunner J. Bartlett, 'interred in France'.

Leaving the church, take the path back to the road and turn left. The road crosses the river and bears right up the hill, reaching Naunton (Baptist) Chapel on the brow. There's another War Memorial here: both this and the one at St Andrew's church are inscribed with the names of the 13 villagers who died in the Great War. From the grounds of the chapel there are fine views of the village and the river. As you stroll along, look out for fossils along window sills and garden paths, the slate roofs made from local stone for which Naunton was once renowned, and a number of old hand-operated water pumps beside the road, which soon descends towards the Black Horse and the centre of the village. Just after the Warden's Way sign on the left, and just before the pub, turn right along Close Hill, cross a bridge over the river and turn right again over a stone stile to walk along the riverbank. Eventually you leave the houses behind, the valley opens out and the village dovecot (27) appears on the right. Turn left here to rejoin the Holst Way.

If time prevents you taking the pleasant Naunton detour, turn right at the bottom of the hill along the Warden's Way into a cul-de-sac alongside a terrace of cottages. The tarmac road soon becomes a grassy path. Beyond the gate marked 'gated road' keep left through the valley, with the village of Naunton above you on the ridge to the left. Soon you arrive at the dovecot.

The Naunton detour rejoins the Holst Way at the clearing described above. Turn right up a steepish path and bear left where it joins a wider path. Continue through a farm gate and take the marked bridle path straight ahead beside Naunton Downs golf course. Continue on this path past the 15th and 17th tees before descending towards the valley. On the way down, swing left at a post with roundels and carry on to the valley floor where you cross a small tributary of the Windrush. Bear right, up to the corner of the last field, cross the stile (or pass through the small gate) onto a road, and continue down the road for about 100m. Pick up the footpath again, as it runs through meadowland with the river on the left. This is the site of the long-abandoned mediaeval village of Lower Harford, whose name has been taken by a nearby farmstead. The mounds at different levels and the long ditch that the footpath crosses are clear evidence of the former settlement, most of which was up the hillside on the other bank of the river.

The route follows the meadows along the valley floor for about one and a half miles, clearly marked as the Winchcombe Way, with the occasional, reassuring Holst Way roundel. Leave the first meadow over a stile beside the right-hand gate. In the middle distance, on the right, are the banks and bridges of the Banbury and Cheltenham Direct Railway. This section was completed in 1881, and Gustav Holst would have been a regular passenger – when funds permitted! - returning home from choir practice and concerts in Bourton-on-the-Water. It hardly needs to be recorded that the line was another victim of the Beeching cuts in 1962.

Just after the path veers away from the river, a Holst Way roundel on a post indicates a right fork and you soon begin a gentle ascent, entering some scrubby woodland. At the top of the incline, turn right through a six-bar gate and walk along the edge of a field to another patch of woodland. After a muddy stretch of about 100m, bear left to emerge from the wood, cross a field and make for the buildings of Aston Farm. Walk through the yard to meet the road that leads to Little Aston Mill **(28)**. At this pretty, sheltered spot the road crosses the Windrush and runs alongside a luxuriantly-planted garden. Then it climbs, becomes a track, and divides at the top of the brow. The long distance Gloucestershire Way (which joined at Little Aston) now strikes off to the left, while the Holst Way continues to the right, along a well-defined path through some attractive natural woodland, then between the wood and a field, and back through the trees again. Railway buffs will be distracted by various relics of the disused line, including a viaduct still in good repair, embankments and a parapet or two. Near the far end of the wood, look out for a section of the perimeter wall on the right which has been smoothed away to create a handy stone 'seat' and 'table' for a refreshment stop, with a fine vantage point over the Windrush Valley. A few paces further on, the path drops downwards and veers right to pass through a wooden gate into open country again.

The lonely stretch of meadow and woodland, running along the resplendent Windrush Valley after Naunton, conveys the impression that little has changed in the last 200 years or so. Houses and farms – even fellow travellers – are a rarity. But it's an illusion: 'civilisation' is fast approaching. As you emerge from the wood and proceed along a grassy path between a hedge and a field, steadily increasing traffic noise indicates the approach of the busy Fosse Way. Once one of the major Roman roads in Britain, stretching for 180 mainly straight miles from Exeter to Lincoln, it is known more prosaically hereabouts as the A429, as it runs into Gustav Holst's teenage haunt of Bourton-on-the-Water.

Bourton-on-the-Water

Pass through a gate, after which the path is firmly enclosed between two fences until it reaches the main road. Cross the road (with great care, because the traffic is fast-moving here) and take the right-hand pavement of a residential street named Lansdown that lies directly ahead and runs alongside the river. After 200m look for the footpath sign that takes the Winchcombe Way to the right; follow this path along the river, across a small common and out between houses to a road.

Turn left on this road and continue to the centre of Bourton. Turn right at the War Memorial and, keeping the river on your right, walk along the green to the far end. With its trickling, shallow waterway and flight of low, arched bridges, busy Bourton has styled itself as the 'Venice of the Cotswolds', and during holiday periods it has flocks of tourists to match. After the solitude and silence of the Windrush Valley, Bourton - lovely as it is - can come as a distinct culture shock.

At the end of the green, continue straight ahead into a shopping street. When you reach the post office, the Holst Way turns left at the junction along Station Road towards the Baptist Church but, before you go any further, a short but important detour is required. Cross the road and walk about 50m to the Old New Inn *(see page 56.)*

From the pub, retrace your steps and turn right along Station Road, passing the Baptist Church and The Manor on your left, until the road bears to the left. Ignore the lane on the right (signposted 'cemetery' and waymarked 'Oxfordshire Way') and take the second turning on the right into Roman Way **(29)**. Turn right again on to a track (Moor Lane) and after a short distance look out for a footpath sign pointing up some steps on the right. Climb the steps over a stile and continue beside the hedge that flanks the track. Cross another stile, and bear right along a path that crosses a stream and leads to a gate. Bear left and pass through a kissing gate at the junction of various paths. Continue straight ahead into the Greystones Nature

Reserve, where an information board near the entrance tells you all you need to know about how this former hay meadow is being returned to nature after decades of gravel extraction and intensive farming. The reserve contains both the Eye and Dikler rivers, and has been classified as a Site of Special Scientific Interest (SSSI).

Follow the waymarked footpath through the reserve, pass another information board announcing a second Nature Reserve, Salmonsbury Meadows, and cross two bridges before emerging into a wide field. Make for a gate in the hedge, cross another bridge and, after going through a second gate, turn left to follow the path between a field and a clump of trees. Continue until you meet the road, and turn right to enter Wyck Rissington.

Village Green
Wyck Rissington

Wyck is the most northerly of three Rissington villages about a mile apart, and two miles south of Stow-on-the-Wold. Its name translates from the Saxon as 'a building of special significance on a hill covered with brushwood': clearly the Saxons were more economical with words than we are! The world is much changed since the Dark Ages, but there's a magical, timeless atmosphere about the hamlet, with its rough and expansive green measuring fully half a mile from end to end, flanked by trim cottages and larger houses from the 17th and 18th centuries, all contending for a place in some Ye Olde England calendar of the future. To complete the idyllic tableau, there's a picturesque duckpond, ornate Victorian drinking fountain and a stand of horse chestnut trees planted for the Coronation in 1953.

Drinking fountain
Wyck Rissington

One of the houses on the green, Maces Cottage, was where Holst lodged during his year as the organist at the village church. He was lent the cottage by the local squire, who described him as "a young man of great promise." Holst supplemented his meagre income of £4 a year by giving music lessons at the cottage.

Wyck Rissington pond

Wyck Rissington's final gem lies directly ahead. Pass the pond and the fountain, and continue for about a quarter of a mile to St Laurence's Church (30) at the southern end of the village. This is a fitting journey's end for the Gustav Holst Way: a perfect place to shed your rucksack, rest your feet and pay homage to the great composer whose love of rambling and the Cotswolds inspired our glorious walk.

St Michael's Church, Guiting Power

Built in Norman times, the church once lay at the centre of the village, but since 1900 twenty or more cottages have disappeared. St Michael's two richly ornamented doors have survived, including the one that forms the main entrance. Other notable features are the beautiful chancel and west window. The foundations of a Saxon chapel have been discovered a short distance to the north: this has been a sacred place for a millennium and a half.

St Michael's fortunes have mirrored those of the village. Agricultural prosperity in the early 19th century increased Guiting's population, and a larger church was needed. The north and south transepts, and the peal of five bells, date from this period. By the end of the century the farming boom was over and both church and village fell on hard times. A full restoration took place in the early 1900s, thanks to the determination of the vicar, who raised funds and managed to preserve the decaying church for future generations.

Naunton Dovecot

Built by the Lord of the Manor around 1600 when doves were valued as meat, the dovecot was restored in 2001 with £90,000 raised by the villagers. The square stone building has 1,176 nest holes, but is no longer used commercially, although numerous birds continue to make use of its facilities. The dovecot is always open both to the elements and visitors; wooden benches in the adjoining storehouse provide a convenient resting place for walkers.

The Old New Inn, Bourton-on-the-Water

Serving the Bourton community since 1714, this atmospheric hostelry originally had an Assembly Room attached. Here the village choral society gave a performance of John Farmer's oratorio *Christ and his Soldiers* in April 1893, conducted by Gustav Holst at the tender age of 18. It is recorded that 'a feature of both chorus and orchestra was the precision and promptitude with which they responded to the conductor's baton […] great praise is due to the talented young Holst.' Some in the choir sensed something very special about the teenage prodigy, and the following year he became Bourton's official choirmaster. A member recalled a typical rehearsal. Holst arrived in the evening gloom carrying 'an old-fashioned stable lantern which he had borrowed at Wyck Rissington to light him on the road to Bourton […] and would catch the last train to Cheltenham.'

St Laurence's Church

Dating from the 12th century, some of the St Laurence's original features remain, notably the buttressed base of the tower (the walls are nine feet thick), the round-arched door between the porch and the vestry, and the tub font, which was buried in the churchyard for many years. The chancel, consecrated in 1269, has one of the earliest known examples of primitive plate tracery. The tower also dates from the 13th century.

St. Laurence's Church
Wyck Rissington

The church has numerous artefacts of note, including ancient glassware showing the total eclipse of the sun in 1322. A wall of the north aisle contains a memorial to the 19 local men who died in the two World Wars. Set into a wall on the left of the chancel, a marble mosaic depicts a maze connecting the fifteen Mysteries of the Gospel. The mosaic commemorates the work of Canon Harry Cheales, who was pastor of St Laurence's from 1947-80. Inspired by a dream, he constructed a real maze in the rectory garden in 1950, which was opened to the public on Coronation Day in 1953. It represents a pilgrim's path through life from cradle to grave, and thence to Heaven. After the Canon's retirement, the rectory was sold and the maze turned into a private garden.

Ravaged by time and weather, St Laurence's roof of Cotswold slate had to be replaced in the early part of this century. The villagers raised the £300,000 required for the restoration, which was completed in the spring of 2011. To mark the achievement, the church commissioned a new limestone cross on the gable end of the church. The central feature is a grill, reflecting the painful experience of St Laurence himself, who was one of the first treasurers of the Church of Rome. In 258AD, the city ordered the Church to hand over its wealth. St Laurence promised to do so within three days, but returned at the appointed hour with the poor and the sick, declaring "This is the Church's treasure." Legend has it that he was then put to death by slow burning on an iron grill. St Laurence is commemorated in a window in the church, and a cottage across the road is named after him.

Remember before God
CANON HARRY CHEALES
who died Sept 3rd 1984 aged 73 years
creator of the original maze and
Rector of this Parish
1947+1980

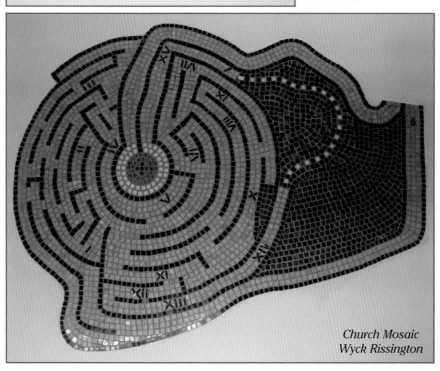

Church Mosaic
Wyck Rissington

Holst at the Rissingtons

Holst was only 17 when he became resident organist at St Laurence's Church, between May 1892 and May 1893 - his first professional engagement. The church organ, a single-manual instrument built in 1871, is still in use today, bearing a commemorative plaque to Holst presented by his many friends in the area. Holst also taught piano and organ to young students at nearby Great Rissington. He used to stay the night at what was the Old Bluecoat School in the village, and often returned to Cheltenham on foot or bicycle. Eventually, painfully cramping neuritis in Holst's right hand put paid to his ambitions to play professionally, so he returned to the trombone he had learnt to play during childhood when his father suggested that the breathing discipline required might cure his asthma. He practised the instrument on many of his walks across the Cotswolds, to the consternation of at least one local farmer, who chased him off his land because he believed the noise was causing his sheep to lamb too early. In 1932, towards the end of his life, Holst walked from Burford to Wyck Rissington to meet a former pupil; then to Bourton-on-the-Water to visit his old friend Cecil Wilkins, before continuing through Winchcombe to Worcester. For a frail man of 58 with numerous physical ailments, this was a remarkable achievement.

Plaque on the wall of the Holst Birthplace Museum

Appendix

Ordnance Survey Maps
Landranger 163
Explorer 45, 179

AA Walker's Map
No 9 (Gloucester and Cheltenham)

Further Reading & Listening

David Bick: *Old Leckhampton (Quarries-Railways-Riots-Devil's Chimney)*, 2nd edition, Runpast Publishing, Cheltenham, 1994.

James Hodsdon: *Pittville Gates – Cheltenham's 'Grand Entrance'* (published by Friends of Pittville, 2011) - available at the Holst Birthplace Museum.

Gustav Holst: *Cotswolds Symphony*, Op. 8, H47 – performed by the Ulster Orchestra, Belfast, October 2011. Naxos 8.572914 (2012) – available at the Holst Birthplace Museum.

Access points and car parks

Cranham: Car parking is available on the common near the church.

Birdlip, Cotswold Way and Crickley Hill: In Birdlip you can park in The George if you ask permission. Between Birdlip and the Air Balloon roundabout there is a public car park reached by turning towards Birdlip from the A417 then taking first right. There is ample parking at Crickley Hill.

Leckhampton Hill and Devil's Chimney: Public car parks can be found in two quarries towards the top of Leckhampton Hill, and off Daisy Bank Road (near Tramway Cottage) at the foot of the hill.

Cheltenham: For the Holst Birthplace Museum park in North Place or Portland St.

Cleeve Hill: Park at the radio masts or, if you take detour 2, at the golf club.

Corndean Lane (near Belas Knap): Park on the roadside opposite the signs up to Belas Knap.

Deadmanbury Gate: It is possible to park on the wide lay-by near the point where the Warden's Way crosses the road from Winchcombe to Guiting Power.

Guiting Manor: Public car parking is available just off Critchford Lane near the Manor House.

Guiting Power: The best parking is by the village hall near the church, which is on the route as you leave Guiting for Naunton.

Bourton-on-the-Water: Plenty of public and private parking available.

Wyck Rissington: No parking is allowed on the green, but roadside parking is permitted.

Tourist Information Centres

Cheltenham: The Wilson Art Gallery & Museum, Clarence Street; 01242 522878

Bourton-on-the-Water: Victoria Street; 01451 820211

Pubs & refreshments

Cranham: Black Horse Inn: 01452 812217

Birdlip: Royal George Hotel: 01452 862506
The Air Balloon: 01452 862541

Crickley Hill Country Park: 01452 863170

National Star College: Star Bistro (closed at weekends): 01242 535984

Cheltenham: various

Prestbury: Plough Inn, Mill Street: 01242 222180
King's Arms, High Street: 01242 244403
Royal Oak, the Burgage: 01242 522344

Cleeve Hill: Cleeve Hill Golf Club: 01242 672025
Rising Sun Hotel: 01242 676281

Guiting Power: Farmer's Arms: 01451 850358
Hollow Bottom Inn: 01451 850392

Naunton: Black Horse Inn: 01451 850565

Bourton-on-the-Water: Old New Inn: 01451 820467

Step inside the Museum and see the piano Holst used to compose *The Planets*. Find out how he developed into a world-class composer by examining and listening to original manuscripts written when he was a schoolboy in Cheltenham. Experience what life was like 'above and below stairs' for his modest middle-class family and their servants through Regency and Victorian period rooms. Imagine yourself as a Victorian child, playing in the nursery. Lose yourself as you listen to the opening bars of *Mars....*

"The most generous-hearted of men - most humble, most noble. He was a prince of musicians and a prince of friends."

Memorial oration by George Bell, Bishop of Chester 1934.

Gustav Holst, one of England's greatest composers, was born in a Regency terraced house in Cheltenham in 1874. The house has been carefully restored and converted into a 'living museum' that captures the atmosphere of the era, both above and below stairs. The most eye-catching of the museum's collection of 3,000 items is the piano on which Holst composed *The Planets*, as popular as ever nearly 100 years after it was published. The museum is at 4 Clarence Road, Cheltenham. Please check the website (www.holstmuseum.org.uk) for times of opening.